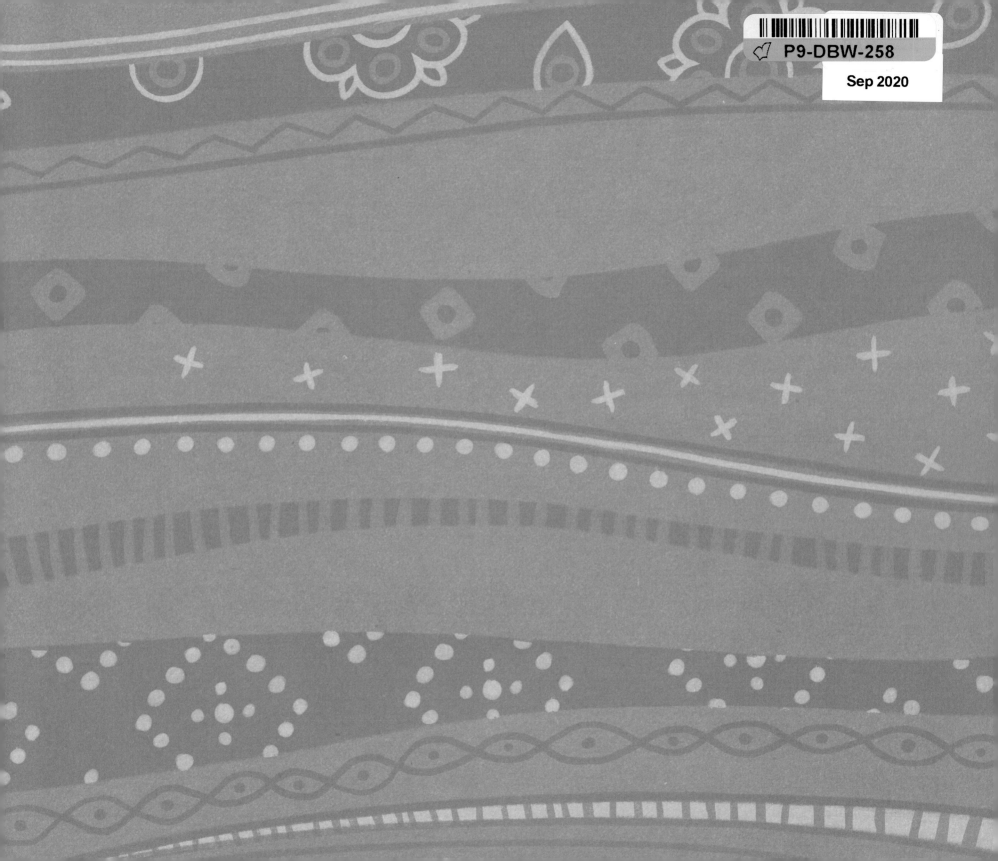

DESERT GIRL, MONSOON BOY

written by
Tara Dairman

illustrated by
Archana Sreenivasan

G. P. PUTNAM'S SONS

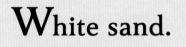

White sand.

Green field.

Light fabric.

Thick shield.

Patterned veil.

Covered hair.

Desert here.

Monsoon there.

Trek for water.

Head to school.

Stitch, embroider.

Learn new rules.

Gather wood.

Home to eat.

Dusty slippers.

Muddy feet.

Flatten dough.

Fingers dip.

Open sky.

Ceiling drip.

Camels rest.
Goats swarm.
Gritty wind.
Rising storm.

Sand blows in.

Flooding floor.

Tie the flap!

Seal the door!

Pack the tents.
   Fill the boats.
Load the camels.
   Lead the goats.

River trickles.
Higher ground.
Thirst quenched.
Dry and sound.

Round the fire,
songs of joy.

Desert girl

and monsoon boy.

AUTHOR'S NOTE

Desert Girl, Monsoon Boy was inspired by people who live and care for their animals in places with extreme dry and wet weather.

In northwest India, the Rabari people (also known as Raika or Rewari) have traditionally led a nomadic lifestyle. Families moving through the dry desert (like the girl's family in the story) must often travel far to find food and water for their herds. For hundreds of years, the Rabari have led their camels to the green slopes of the Aravalli Range, east of the desert, to take advantage of the rains that fall there.

Today, more and more Rabari are giving up their nomadic ways to settle in permanent homes (like the boy's family). This shift brings many changes. Children may be able to go to school for the first time, but families may have to get rid of many of their animals and find other work to support themselves.

Even people who live in villages are not always safe from the weather. The rainy season—called monsoon—can cause dangerous flash floods. In recent years, flooding has forced entire villages in this part of India to evacuate. People fleeing the floods must take all their belongings (including goats and other animals) with them as they move to higher, safer ground.

This story imagines a nomadic family in search of water and a village-dwelling family seeking to escape it. Perhaps their paths would cross in the Aravalli hills, and together they would celebrate their safety.

Their meeting is a work of fiction. But as our climate changes, extreme conditions like drought and flooding will continue to put the lives of people and animals in this part of the world in very real danger.

Several international nonprofit and nongovernmental organizations (NGOs) address the needs of pastoralists with an eye toward long-term sustainability. If you would like to learn more about the work that these groups are doing, a good place to start is www.pastoralpeoples.org/partners. Please consider joining me in supporting organizations such as these around the world.

—*Tara Dairman*

ILLUSTRATOR'S NOTE

The visual representation of the two families in this book are based on two different groups of the Rabari people—the girl's from Gujarat, and the boy's from Rajasthan. I was fascinated by the fact that each Rabari group follows its own distinct practices with regard to living spaces, apparel, textiles, jewelry, and other details. Many years ago, I had the opportunity to visit a Rabari settlement in Rajasthan, where I got to see how organized their settlements were and how they wasted absolutely nothing. They welcomed me into their homes, served me delicious meals, and allowed me to explore their spaces with my camera. My research for this book allowed me to spend hours poring over photos and articles about both groups, and they continue to inspire me. I'm very glad to have had a chance to illustrate this book!

—*Archana Sreenivasan*

Thank you to the team at Lokhit Pashu-Palak Sansthan (LPPS), a nonprofit organization in Rajasthan, India, that supports Raika camel pastoralists, for providing feedback on this book at various points in its production process, helping ensure that its words and art reflect their world as accurately as possible. It has been a privilege to have their input on this story.

For all who journey —T.D.

To Mother Earth and
her ancient wisdom —A.S.

G. P. PUTNAM'S SONS
An imprint of Penguin Random House LLC, New York

G. P. Putnam's Sons is a registered trademark of Penguin Random House LLC.

Visit us online at penguinrandomhouse.com

Library of Congress Cataloging-in-Publication Data
Names: Dairman, Tara, author. | Sreenivasan, Archana, illustrator.
Title: Desert girl, monsoon boy / Tara Dairman; illustrated by Archana Sreenivasan.
Description: New York, NY: G. P. Putnam's Sons, [2020] | Summary: "Two families flee
extreme weather in India and come together on a mountaintop"—Provided by publisher.
Identifiers: LCCN 2019029824 (print) | LCCN 2019029825 (ebook) | ISBN 9780525518068 (hardcover) |
ISBN 9780525518075 (ebook) | ISBN 9780525518082 (kindle edition)
Subjects: CYAC: Family life—India—Fiction. | Sandstorms—Fiction. | Monsoons—Fiction. | India—Fiction.
Classification: LCC PZ8.3.D1364 Des 2020 (print) | LCC PZ8.3.D1364 (ebook) | DDC [E]—dc23
LC record available at https://lccn.loc.gov/2019029824
LC ebook record available at https://lccn.loc.gov/2019029825

Manufactured in China by RR Donnelley Asia Printing Solutions Ltd.
ISBN 9780525518068
10 9 8 7 6 5 4 3 2 1

Design by Eileen Savage and Nicole Rheingans | Text set in Carre Noir Std
The art for this book was drawn in pencil and painted digitally.